GW01454161

# GENERIC HUSBAND

# REBECCA HAZELTON

POEMS

# GENERIC

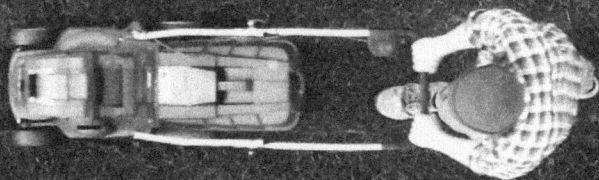

# HUSBAND

LOUISIANA STATE UNIVERSITY PRESS
BATON ROUGE

Published by Louisiana State University Press
lsupress.org

Copyright © 2025 by Rebecca Stafford
All rights reserved. Except in the case of brief quotations used in articles or reviews,
no part of this publication may be reproduced or transmitted in any format or by
any means without written permission of Louisiana State University Press.

LSU Press Paperback Original

Designer: Kaelin Chappell Broaddus
Typefaces: Quadraat OT, text; Dharma Gothic, display
Cover images: (front) Adobe Stock/Big Shot Theory,
(back) Adobe Stock/Ljupco Smokovski

Library of Congress Cataloging-in-Publication Data

Names: Hazelton, Rebecca, 1978– author
Title: Generic husband : poems / Rebecca Hazelton.
Other titles: Generic husband (Compilation)
Description: Baton Rouge : Louisiana State University Press, 2025.
Identifiers: LCCN 2025018296 (print) | LCCN 2025018297 (ebook) | ISBN
    978-0-8071-8472-1 (paperback) | ISBN 978-0-8071-8566-7 (epub) | ISBN
    978-0-8071-8567-4 (pdf)
Subjects: LCSH: Husbands—Poetry | LCGFT: Poetry
Classification: LCC PS3608.A9884 G46 2025 (print) | LCC PS3608.A9884
    (ebook) | DDC 811/.6—dc23/eng/20250611
LC record available at https://lccn.loc.gov/2025018296
LC ebook record available at https://lccn.loc.gov/2025018297

*for Mark*

# CONTENTS

# GENERIC HUSBAND

## More Husbands

The husbands have a plan. The plan is to make
more husbands. More husbands, more problems,
is a thing the husbands have never said.
The more husbands there are the more husbands
there will be. Husbands beget husbands.
The cities will be full of husbands. Husbands will spill
from the upper stories of apartment buildings.
Husbands will clog the canals of Amsterdam.
Husbands will walk across the Grand Canyon
on the bodies of other husbands.
There will be so many husbands
that husbands will seem interchangeable.
One husband is much like another husband
in the dark. Even now, the orchards are full
of husbands, ripening in the afternoon sun.
The farmers' market sells fresh, young
husbands every spring. But artisanal husbands
are not cost-effective. The husbands are building
a factory to modernize the making of husbands.
Now every husband working the line
has their hands on just one part of another
husband in production. Some of the beauty
of creation is lost, but speed is everything.
One day a husband will ask his husband
to get him a glass of water, and that husband
will pause over the kitchen sink, looking out
the window. He'll see a wild husband
furtively slink across the front yard,
then duck out of sight into a culvert.
*There but for the grace of God*, says
the husband, but he shivers all the same.

# Trompe l'Oeil

Say the husband was one of a series. Say a barcode discretely
stamped on the inside of his lower lip gave his model number,
and that model number was discontinued. The current model
performs its daily tasks without issue. The eggs are scrambled
in a shallow pool of hot butter, sprinkled with flakes of salt
by the husband's clever hands. It took a team of engineers five years
to perfect the way the husband flips the lid on the salt cellar—that panache
doesn't come cheap. This model is highly rated by consumers.
There were several women who wanted to retain the husband
and his services, but the husband's licensing is limited
to five to ten years. For five to ten years the husband will love
you for the rest of his memory. The best of his ability
is a certainty when memory isn't. What are most astonishing
are the details that hardly matter—the way his hair falls out of place
while he recharges or the ingrown toenail that inflames
at six-month intervals. It's these needless imperfections
that throw the higher functions into bright relief.
The way he has of joking until you crack out of your black mood.
The way he will carry a heavy load and then ask for more weight.
Say the model is discontinued. Say you go on as before and ignore
the recall notice. Say he tries to make a joke but the punchline
is a file not found. Say one day he falls while in the garden—hardly
a fall at all—and then won't acknowledge voice commands.
Say he's a blank screen. Say he's bricked. It's here that the conceit
falls to pieces. There's no system error. The plants in the garden
grow with or without tending. Your husband is dead.

## Optimistic Husband

There is, in the center of the woods, a man
                                    of white marble, surrounded
                        by a creeping green,
                whose gold-flecked forearms
            are flexed in the act
                    of holding something that is no longer
                                there, whose trunk
            is a muscled column of resistance,
                    whose legs strain
        to lift the body from an earth
                                that every year claims another inch,
                    green on the calves.
Summer is summer
                    and there is always greener
        creeping the small of the back, creeping green
                        in the straining neck,
                lining the eyes green,
                    the idea of the green
                                creeping.
Whoever carved the man
                had some idea
        of what it is to suffer
                a longing
        that is never answered,
                            to be beautiful
                but still not enough.
A serious man strains
        against the silent season.
A foolish man
        thinks the struggle is certainty.
                                The green
                advances, seeping indifference
                            into the cracks
                    of everything.

The summer stretches
                    into a landscape of its own.
      The man still stands.

## The Husband's Answers

The images don't explain a story. They are a counterpoint.

It's understandable to mistake them for metaphor, but still, a mistake.

The trouble comes from thinking. I could stop there. The trouble comes from thinking an image *is* a story.

This is how painting began. Little glimpses into little worlds. Little glimpses into the faces of the divine.

But we know that the gods don't really look like us.

Yes, all Western art.

I can't speak to that.

Berger says the image, disconnected from a fixed location, proliferates, and changes through new context, strange juxtapositions, reframing.

What they do to us, yes. The stories they tell us, and how we accept those stories.

He is less interested in the stories we bring.

If I show you an image of a bird flying, you might think *freedom*, or *graceful*, or *wings*. You might remember your mother pointing to the sky, naming the bird *starling, heron, crow*. But all of that is yours.

The bird is just the bird, flying, following the magnetic fields of the earth home.

I did not say the trouble was a bad thing. I only said that it was trouble.

# Epithalamium, Winter Palace

*with a line from Catullus*

No easy palm is set out for us, comrades.
The Winter Palace we would storm is fortified
rococo, and outside the city there are animals
bleached to match their context. When we strapped on
our boots this morning, we could not know the implications
of their smart shine or predict the path
they would carve in the snow. In the future,
our wives will release us from these constrictions.
But until our wives are our wives, we are just men
marching, and in marching we are defined
against our context as knives drawn
define themselves against all that would stay
their course. The construction has been razed
and burned and rebuilt, but the floor plan remains
the same. It is only the people that change
the furnishings to keep in step with the latest
dance—and so we put away our mead and vodka
for champagne and burgundy, slur
our accents to a more pleasing elision, paste jewels
to the easing stool. Is function still function
when it glitters? Once we pass through these iron
gates we will be different men; we will be bleached
to match our content. Our wives are waiting
with the hands we've waited for, the ones that can
pop a buckle and release us from these shoes
that keep us restless, that hide our bloody socks.

## Generic Husband

Who mows the lawn. Who prunes the rangy rose.
Who whacks the weeds by the chain link with mafioso panache.
Who drinks the beer. Who has no questions. Who knots
a tie four-in-hand. Who washes the car. Who drives stick.
Who smoked but did not inhale. Who wears the drugstore cologne
his kid gave him. Who wakes up beside the same wife.
Who has no questions. Who parts his hair. Who has a bald patch.
Who plays golf. Who plays Call of Duty. Who plays
the stock market, responsibly. Who reads biographies
of generals. Who does not dream. Who climbed trees
as a boy. Who leaves his towel beside the hamper.
Who has never swum nude. Who knows cardinal directions.
Who sees the sun set without a sense of unease.
Who walks to the train. Who watches sports. Who reclines.
Who maintains a sense of calm. Who has a small, bad tattoo.
Who wears humorous socks. Who tells the tame dirty joke.
Who reads the newspaper online. Who is politically unmoved.
Who had a job upon graduation. Who go-gets. Who has no questions.
Who shovels the walk. Who did not keep his letters
from his college sweetheart. Who had a college sweetheart.
Who called her "baby." Who was sincere. Who did not ask
why she left him. Who does not climb trees. Who drinks one beer
at the end of the day. Who remembers meeting his wife and how young
she was then. Who does not question. Who kills the spider.
Who clips a dog with his car and keeps driving. Who adjusts the mirror.

## Specific Husband

The world was sick and he couldn't fix it
                so he gathered deadfall
                                into a pile in the backyard.
*He? You mean, you?* Yes. He had a plan
                and a reciprocating saw.
He cut larger into smaller.
                        He stabbed the ground
          with the sharpened ends of the thicker branches
until they sunk,
             and those were his supports.
The more pliant, thinner branches
                  he wove between the poles.
*Did it help?* It did not help.
                    Surfaces still had to be wiped, uselessly.
                    Masks worn. The news poured in
                    and filled his home to the brim
                    with wet leaves.
Whole countries became sick.
               Cities became sick.
                  His wife became sick.
                      He could not fix it.
Sometimes he reinforced the weaving
with twine. Other times, he used the pressure
             of one branch against another,
the way his wife had provided a resistance
             that was also a support.
*This is still you.* Yes.
    *What were you making?* It was a basket
                  that couldn't hold.
                  It was a deer's nest.
*Then what?* He laced the softest
          branches into a canopy
          through which one could see
          the true canopy above.

When his wife was weak he would carry her
to what he'd made and lay her inside.
*Did it help?* It did not help.
But it did not hurt, either.
She was an egg inside a nest.
He monitored her oxygen.
He monitored her speech for slurring.
*Did she hatch?* No.
The months dragged in snow.
The snow turned the structure
into a lace collar. Wind blew through.
Then daffodils pricked out everywhere.
Then crocuses.
The structure was still standing.
He trimmed the border with a weedwhacker
and let the grass inside grow long.
He trained vines over it,
and one day it erupted
into a tangle of petals, tendrils, tender leaves.
*And then she got better?*
He dismantled it. She is still sick.

## The Husband as Mentalist

Think of a number.
        Hold in your mind the age you were
when you first realized
           your body couldn't be trusted
to take care of you.
            Maybe the first kiss, that boy
with a penknife, or maybe
        what came after.
            Maybe it was the bleeding
every month and then the month you didn't.
                Or the running
        leap and the short fall marked,
the pebble gravel spraying.
Or the bike tumbling
           into the ditch and the long gash
           in the leg's meat.
The moment can vary.
The tells don't.
        The way your mouth moves
        and I follow.
How you toss
your hair, as if to say,
         *Just get on with it.*
But waiting
is something I'd like
           to teach you, just like I'd like
to teach you how to touch without touching,
        how I know
        which door you'll walk through
             before you do,
the way you sweeten your coffee
           until it's syrup.
Lying is wrong, and so I always tell you
the truth

about why you want
the things you want.

              The easiest thoughts to find
           are the ones that mean
       something, if only to you.


When you got up from that ditch
          your sock was red with blood.
You walked home
       because you knew
         no one was coming, and the cars passed
with their bright headlights,
                en route to warm houses
         where mothers pick up on the first ring
           and fathers carry
            girls with scraped knees home.
Maybe you didn't know
       your own number and that's why
    no one answered.
It *was nothing*, you say,
       but nothing is also a number.

## The Husband Was Once a Teenaged Boy

was long in limb
                   was finely turned
                                fingers on the steal
was careless
           because beautiful
                        was hurtful
                                   because heartless
is heartless

              was a child in a man's body
was a girl
in a passport photo
                    was a brash tiger lily
                       from his mother's garden

                                        was severe
                         when his mates were antic
was reserved
and monochrome
                was in love

       but not enough

was approached
on the beach to model
                   was approached in a bar
                                    to model
was approached
by an older man
             to model
                           everything was modeling

everything was easy

was careless
his beauty
was a lodestar
to himself

was singular
was strange
was heartless

## The Husband Has a Dream

The streetlights in the cul-de-sac
             blinked on one by one, illuminating
       the husband's grief as it rose and fell
in radiant clouds of dust, settling on the morning
             glories clamped tight against the night,
    on his suit jacket,
    on the backs of his hands.
                   If he tried to brush it away
             it smeared him with greasy soot,
                      so he didn't try.
All around him were houses
       whose windows poured golden light
                   onto the lawns
and inside each room
       small dramas enacted.

In one, parents floated
    around the dinner table, desperate
             to keep a child laughing.
In another, a man fucked a bored woman
       on the stairs and with every step
             she slipped further away.
A teenaged boy read a book and drank his first beer.
A dog slept alone by the fire.

       It seemed to the husband
             that someone must be waiting
    for him to come home, but
       there were no keys in his pockets.

             By then there was so much dust
       in the air that it almost seemed solid before him,
             forming a frame,
             then a door, then a lock.

The hardest part was grasping the handle—
       which was suffering—
              and then he was through.

## The Husband's Answers

As an abstraction, yes. The way the physical world reminds us that there might be something better, elsewhere. There is a chair, and somewhere, a better chair. There was the image of her in the garden, pulling weeds, and somewhere, a better woman, a better garden.

If you believe in that sort of thing.

I don't believe in tarot, but I like the art. I have five decks. I bought them all myself, which is against the rules. I like pulling a card as a diagnostic tool. If the card makes me flinch, it's probably right.

I would start the film here, with these questions.

There was a time when I wanted so badly for my art to speak to others. Now I am speaking only to myself, and it is better that way.

Again, as an abstraction. But it's not something that can be seen clearly. Like how teenaged American girls giggle at the statues of Vestal Virgins in Rome. They can only understand how they have viewed virginity.

To wield it as power—impossible.

Yes, Rome. I bought gelato and the man handing it to me took my finger and pressed it into the cold dessert, staring at me all the while.

Perhaps because American. Perhaps he wanted me. That was not unusual.

It's a moment like any other, in that it feels meaningful, and it comes to nothing.

There are exceptions.

# The Interior of the Husband

is sometimes a room
                    painted green, and other times
        a spoon
            sucked clean,
                    the silver smell of it
            and the tin taste remaining,

is rarely the unlit nave of a church
                        lined in velvet smoke
            from swinging censers,

is hardly ever a freshly scrubbed washtub
                with a whimsical drain cover.

If sometimes
                on a clear, ice-cracked day
he places one boot before
                        the other with particular care,

        it is not because a china tea set
                        is balanced on a too small table
                                    inside him,
it is not
because he is lined with windchimes
            and trying to be silent.

He walks to the train station, boards,
                and sets his face
                    to match the blank surroundings.

The beauty of the exterior
                is that it needn't reveal
                    the beneath.

The outside of the train
is limned
in thin ice.
Inside is all
hot breath and steam.

## The Husband with Clothes

Who doesn't like a bit of flash,
                        a pop of red
                                like a nosebleed
                dribbling down a crisp white shirt?
To catch the eye requires a touch
        of violence
                that spreads along threads like a bloom.

But if the clothes make the man, then the man
        is already unmade. A man like that is one loose thread
                away from annihilation.

So it is that the silhouette of my body
                        in our bedroom
                is like a gate
                swung open to the darkness
        I button up every morning,
so it is that I tug my cuffs
                        until a slice of white
                appears, just enough
                        to signal my attention to detail.

## Husband Paraphrase

The husband had long suspected himself
                    of happiness. When he looked askance
at his life, at his wife, at the lilies
                she'd planted alongside the garage,
he felt a disappointing peace.

                    Where were the beautiful beasts
                    he'd sought, sword in hand,
                        his horse a steady current
                            beneath him?

Where was the woman
of singular perfume, whose touch
                sent him swooning
into dreams of sensual violence?

Nothing flogged him
            to his satisfaction.
The flags on his castle
            were limp.

One night, when all the children had dispersed
                    from the long, bourgeois lawns,
                            after his wife hardened into sleep
                    and fell beyond his reach,

he stepped from the porch
                into the night, heroic.
Nothing stirred in the backyard,
or in his chest. His dreams cooled,
                        gelatinous.

Now, looking back, he saw that the small white house he'd left
                                was a line drawing on a scrim,

the grass a series of waves
in a cardboard sea,
the lilies ruddy glassine,
and the song he'd sung thin as a cricket's scrape.

Women emerged from the trees
at the edge of the lawn,
naked,
wild, their bodies
smeared with wine, mud, with the singular
perfume of blood.

They did not like his song.
He was not a faun.
They pulled at him until he tore,
then pulled some more.

In the house, his wife
turned over, her dreams
scented with heavy lilies, unaware
of her husband's
unbearable joy.

## Glazed Case

Dear husbands you hardly know how to set the green
growing you hardly know the vine and its tremors
the whispers of plants are a subtext I mean subterranean
I mean a terrarium is a larger world made small
and manageable if light if soil if the ratio of wet
to dry is a golden afternoon and the way a husband
lies down for a moment in the grass the sun spilling
across his thinning hair the shirt open his eyes closed
then dear husbands lust is easy and life is a seed
in a Styrofoam egg crate if we are patient
two green paddles split the soil's dark waters
if we are patient the husband will rise again to finish
mowing the lawn he will not leap over the fence
in one graceful vault looking for a moment dear husbands
like something unaccountable to a closed system

## The Husband as Tilda Swinton in Most Anything

Like an ermine looping through the snow, mouth a pink line,
      I'm suited for my habitat. I disappear into the white drift
and blue tint of a petticoat as easily as I suit up into slim
      trousers, breasts bound and hair slicked.
I have been an angel. I have been a dog. I have been most
      of the high notes in a choir, and once I was even
the clicking sound in your jaw in the morning. I'm versatile.
      I'm a dream of a man if a man was a woman and
if that woman had a dream of stepping out of the dark forest
      at night and walking to the lake's edge
and the moons, one in the sky, one in the water,
      were the same as she remembered from when she was young
and every gesture was her own and no one else's.
      Then someone called her name, and she stepped
into that name and ever since I've had all manner of roles,
      none of them as strange as this one.

## The Husbands Are Running

the husbands are running over hill over dale the husbands are running

they run the husbands are running they vault picket fences the husbands

are running the husbands pump their arms the husbands loosen

their ties the husbands are running they run the husbands' cufflinks

are dropping like bullets the husbands are running they leap over

boxwoods the husbands are running the husbands they run they kick off

their shoes they hop off their socks they run the belts are slithering

and flying away the husbands are running the husbands

race the dogs howl the husbands they run the backyards are full

of the husbands running the husbands call to the husbands to run

the husbands are running they run the husbands drop trousers

the husbands in boxers the husbands in briefs the husbands are running

the button-downs unbuttoning the husbands are running the hair

receding and the paunch is rising the husbands are running they run

the husbands on statins the husbands gone vegan the husbands

with heart stents the husbands are running they run the husbands

run ragged the husbands run weary they run golden in the fading light

the sun retreating the husbands are running the husbands they run

the husbands as one the husbands the husbands they run

## The Husband's Answers

Say there is a room.

We can see that room in the past, and we can see that room in the future.

The room stays the same.

It's the people walking through who differ.

The people in the future room want to know what happened in the past room.

The people in the past room can only imagine the people in the future room.

The room stays the same.

The people in the past room write letters to the people in the future room.

This is how the people in the future room know about the people in the past room.

There is no way to write to the people in the past room, of course.

The room stays the same.

The people in the past room describe their lives in their room.

They can't know if the people in the future room will understand them.

The people in the future room read the letters.

Our problem is, we aren't in either room.

## The Husband's Legerdemain

When I show you
                what I'm working with, you should assume
the real props are unseen.
             When I pretend to light
     this short pencil
it's to disguise the cigarette
          smoking in my ear, just out of sight.
               We see what we expect,
and I know a hot cherry
        from a dull lead,
      just as I know the difference between
            a want and a need.
   Clarity is what we want.
      Lying is what we need.

A single finger's pad
      can be so sensitive;
                the ridge of a print can pop
a card from its mates
      or make a crooked deck seem square.
My grip is standard, except
        when you straddle me,
then I am a dealer
     with a fan flourish, stripping
from the top.

     The white border of a card can conceal
a faulty double lift,
      the way a white dress lifting
        off your body
      on a hotel bed
while I am waiting
at home for your call
      camouflages taking more than you deserve.

This kind of magic is intimate. An open hand has no secrets
                    that can't be disguised
through locking eyes.
       The trick requires you to see
                       how much I want you to believe
and then forget
         how much you want the same thing.

  Again and again, I remind you
        to watch
            what the other hand is doing.
          Let me show you what you want to see.
I promise never to do the same trick twice.
       I promise never to explain.

## The Husband Sees Clearly

                    I can't forget
the softness that Bernini fakes,
          how the thigh is just as firm as the hand
                              pressing down.
All day I question what it means
              to find another beautiful, knowing that beauty
resists apprehension.

I told myself my desire
          was justified
          because it was mine,

          but I only want to tell you just enough
              to satisfy and seal your idea of me
          behind a hermeneutic glass.
                    Isn't preservation a form of worship?

I am tired of creating. Making and making
                    until nothing can be made more.

                    Instead, I think about thinking,
          the soft mouse fur
                    lining your winter coat's pocket,
anything gentler
than the ugly eroticism of the grasping hand.

          Let me instead recreate
          a scene from our first year, when we were liquid
                    over a jar's lip,
when we were always drunk
              on vodka, chocolate, gloriously crispy chicken skin,
when the words
          *I love you* tumbled out of my mouth
                    two weeks in,

and I waited in the dark
    for you to say
        a matching phrase.

*I love you.* What a terrible idea!
        Decades later, I'm still waiting,
   my hand still
        pressed to your flesh,
my devotion
terrible, beautiful, unrelenting.

## Things the Husband Will Not Say

Here is the old feeling again—
                hunger in the body
and nowhere to put it.
                But the old feeling is new
                      every time, and every time
              I forget what it is
          to believe in its satisfaction.

     Some people
have a persistent sadness
        that stains them
through and through,
              like a man's hands
                tinged the color of an old Bible
        after decades of smoking.
They have a hurt and layer it
           with nacre until it's a bulbous pearl—
but it's still the same accident, covered over.

           It's like that with desire—
                    I push it down
            and up it comes again
                years later, refined
           darker, more lustrous.

I am speaking
metaphorically.
          I am not speaking drastically.

If I tell you I want
          what you cannot give me,
     you will fail to try to try.

Or worse, you will,
and I can't bear to see you
once more awkward
in a harness, gamely locking in
a ridiculous purple dildo.

When I say I'm hungry,
I mean there was a man
in a bathroom in Glasgow
who understood me
well enough,
and sometimes I miss the men
whose names I never knew.
But I love you,
mostly, and mostly, I can compress this feeling
into a tight diamond for your hand.
We are years away
from talking
without metaphors.

## Apocalypse, Again

At first, it's nothing but killing, and taking,
but once fucking enters, bartering comes in,
and then other acts for other objects, and my husband
assures me that in this new economy he'll be in demand
as a man who can throw a pot, because eventually,
we will want to eat things out of containers again,
and not just put our jaws to a fresh kill;
we'll cook again, which will remind us we are more
than the lion faces we wear, and not immediately, but eventually,
we might even want a little beauty, and he can make that, too.
Because my husband loves me, he promises he will keep me
in the back of his tent should my glasses break, which they will,
though I'll wear them for years past their prescription and stare
through the star pattern on the left eye, where a marauder clubbed me
upside the temple. My husband promises he will keep me in the back of his tent
and I can wedge clay, or pick through lentils if there are lentils,
that might be too advanced, agriculturally, I just don't know
if I can be trusted with a knife to gut animals I can't see,
and anyway, it's in the tent he keeps me, and that's a lot of blood.
For some things there is no fix. We talk about this at parties.
We are forming plans. Our friend Windham envisions zombies
as what brings us all down. He advocates a Home Depot
as base of operations because there are forklifts, fencing, and generators.
You could build a sort of life out of zip ties and American know-how.
We could rebuild and pretend that it's different. Still, I think it's more likely
my husband will be running through the forest, if we can find a forest,
and that his feet will be soundless, and the deer will just walk up to him, meekly,
and let him slit their throats, because we will be hungry,
and this is what happens to meek things when there is no future.

## The Husband's Answers

I had forgotten about death.

Personally, I live my life deliberately. I spend hours composing answers in my mind.

Transcribing them is difficult. There's no intention to it. The language is flawed.

The deadly classicism of certain buildings. Not the original Parthenon. But government buildings that borrow its authority. Post offices. Municipal courts. Oppressive.

And then the sprawling houses, built in the suburbs for day traders and patent lawyers.

The Parthenon was Athena's first, then Mary's, then a mosque.

Tourists. Now it belongs to tourists.

In the folds of the white marble, there is the bare trace of the brightest color.

A child can be a mistake, but inevitable.

## Foolish Husbands

Youthful husbands on the cliff's edge,
                              husbands followed
by tiny, yapping dogs. Husbands faithful

to intercession. Husband zero. Husbands on adventures,
husbands without
maps. Optimistic husbands sans doubts.

Trusting husbands. Playful husbands. Art brut husbands.
                                        Self-taught husbands.
Untrained husbands and untrained dogs.

Ragged husbands with feathers in their hair, their beards.
Wild husbands
with wild dogs tearing their stockings. Husbands carrying bindles.

Husbands carrying roses. Husbands of the unexamined life.
                              Husbands forever
full of potential. Everyman husbands clothed

in their ridiculous bodies. Archetypal husbands.
Blank-slate husbands
and trick husbands and excuse husbands.

Husbands as protagonists journeying through the world.
                              Crocodile husbands crying
crocodile tears. Extravagant husbands spending

the rent, manic husbands giving away their winter coats,
husbands on the precipice,
husbands stepping out into the nothing, confident.

## The Husband without Clothes

Admit it. This is how you want me, slick
where desired,
rough where requested.
       Seamless in the dark.
Muscle
is a product of resistance,
    sinews a measure of tension,
and you love the interplay
     of both under your hands.
It's not so hard
   to be what you want
     when what you want
      is simple.
It's enough
when it's enough, and by this metric
we have brought ourselves to the hours
 between
  blue dusk and glaring dawn
    in a world that doesn't want us
      wholly satisfied.
If the present is a weed
   cracking the asphalt,
then the past is an errant seed.


      Isn't it strange to speak
      these words?
I shudder and the birds lift
  from the trees
outside our bedroom window.
     You laugh and they come back,
      preen and settle.
It has been like this for years,
my enemy,
my love.

I am with you in the waver and wilderness
                              of the decades.
I am standing by the bed
                    at full attention. I am listening
to the story you tell with your body's bewildered hitch

          and catch, the change

that unbraids the self
    from itself,
              for a time,
                    effortless.

## Crypto Husbands

Husbands are a rising commodity.
> Husbands are unregulated.

Husbands are decentralized.
> There's nothing husbands love more

than telling you about the distribution of husbands.
> It takes many husbands to validate

a husband. If a husband is validated,
> the reward is more husbands.

Creating more husbands is not ecologically sound.
> The ownership of husbands

requires a study of secrets.
> The study of secrets is classified

as a weapon in some countries.
> All the husbands want is to communicate

under adversarial conditions.
> If Alice sends Bob a message, it's best

for everyone that Eve does not know.
> The more husbands are praised

the more husbands are in demand.
> The value of husbands is inconstant.

At times, they are equal to desire.
> Other times, they are outstripped

by demand. Transactions with husbands
> are irreversible. If the key to a husband

is lost, so is the husband.

## Useful Tragedy

It's an old story,
       how she stepped from the house
              to the backyard,
and then farther
           to the trees beyond,
      to the bank of the distant river
where they found her later.
              Her damp hair
shone bright against the black, wet dirt,
the green moss
grew over her muddy shoulder,
               and her smeared mouth
                  was the color
                     of anything.
Finally, she was ready
       to be fought for:
for a husband
     who'd sing her return,
until death and dogs did cry,

      until the stairs arranged themselves before him
with a slice of sunlight at the top,
       like a lemon peel floating
           on a dry Manhattan—

but this is not his story. Or hers, really.

      This is the story of reason
    and how it argues so convincingly
      against hope
         until we turn too quickly,
     and see the departing wave
of the very chance
        for which we'd prayed.

# The Husband Considers Beauty

Suffering doesn't make us beautiful, but every time
                    I'm hungover
          some woman hands me a card
and suggests I take off my shirt,
               especially if I am in The City,
               especially if I am next to an elegant man
        whose cigarette hangs off his lip.
                      Jimin's better looking
            but my face has the touching vulnerability
                     of nausea,
the kind of open-faced sweetness
           that could sell Americans a few thousand
        midcentury couches.

Have I ever considered modeling?
             I can't remember when I last shaved.

            When I was twenty and my hair was long
     I was regularly mistaken on campus
           for a rugby player named Chloe.
When I eventually met Chloe at a party
        she was angry with me
           for looking so much like her.
Perhaps, I said, we are just terribly gorgeous and also
                  in a Russian novel.

Jimin's pants cost $800
       before alterations.
           When he walks,
      he adds to the beauty
         of the street, where a cold wind
    whips the leaves and trash

                        into patterns
            that aren't,
because it's the randomness that pains us.

Finally, I am no longer young.

## The Husband Proposes

A girl like you,
        reclining on your elbows,
           wearing nothing
               but a black cowboy hat, pleased
              to be so thoroughly
               yourself,
what can I do but take thee?

I take thee behind the barn
           while the barn cat circles,
      I take thee against a bureau
           and every drawer applauds,
I take thee
    stoned
      and generous
in the woods behind
          the pasture,
             I take thee drunk
                 in our first apartment's shower,
          pulling the towel bar down,
        losing my deposit.

      And yes, I take thee while you still love another
        more than I'd like,
so I take thee to the courthouse
         and request a record
of the missionary position

because your mouth
is a counterfeit
        I'll spend and spend,
and you blush because you cannot
       blush sincerely.

You are so thoroughly yourself,
            and in that way,
always naked.
                Place that Stetson on your head
                                    just so,
            I take thee as you were
        and as you are,
                and forge my name to yours.

## The Husband's Answers

Out at the edge of the dark lawn. She is swinging on the tire swing, barely visible but for her white dress, the motion of the constant near miss.

When she has had enough of the violet dusk, enough of being alone, she'll return.

She'll return, but the form she wears won't be the same.

A fear, sharp as a misplaced pin.

The bats flying overhead, the few and fewer lightning bugs, the crickets' invocations—I might forget all of it.

The fir tree fragrant and looming.

What did she look like when she stepped from the house to the lawn?

A white heron picking its way across a black lake.

I do not want to forget.

If I do, I do not want to know.

## The Husband at Rest

Now am I as the century
        unwinding, the lustrous
    past sifted from our present grind.
             Vast, matter of fact,
    painful in the fine and particulate.

You think I am steady
breath, steady hands,
      a man who has no desire to take
  from trouble.

You think I am
    a man who is held to a line.

Today you told me
      of one more reason not to love you
and the telling was a bell
      ringing out the joy of its own cracking.
         Now we know
        what you're made of.
Now we can see inside.

     Night is closing on our small backyard,
and the bats ring the sky
     in widening schools of black scrap.
You are somewhere in the gold box
       at the top of the hill,
moving objects
   from room to room.

No matter how I try,
    I cannot forget how long
    I've held the world above my head.

Its weight feels like your body
              after you've fallen asleep
           beside me: dense, vacant, and imperative.


           Loneliness is a complete calculation.
What we are equal to
isn't the same.


           There are whole calendars
where you crossed off the days,
                      assured
that more were coming.
              I see with a longer view.

## My Husband

My husband in the house.
　　　　　My husband on the lawn,
pushing the mower, Fourth of July, the way
　　　　　my husband's sweat wends like Crown Royale
to the waistband
of his shorts,
　　　　　the slow-motion shake of the head the water
running down his chest,
　　　　　all of this lit like a Warrant video
Cherry Pie his cutoffs his blonde hair his air guitar crescendo.
My husband
at the PTA meeting.
　　　　　My husband warming milk
　　　　　at 3:00 a.m.
　　　　　while I sleep.
My husband washing the white Corvette the bare chest and the soap,
　　　　　the objectification of my husband
by the pram pushers
and mailman.
　　　　　My husband at Home Depot asking
where the bolts are,
　　　　　the nuts, the screws,
my god, it's filthy
　　　　　my husband reading from the news,
　　　　　my husband cooking French toast, Belgian waffles,
my husband for all
nationalities.
　　　　　My husband with a scotch, my husband
with his shoes off,
　　　　　his slippers on, my husband's golden
leg hairs in the glow of a reading lamp.
My husband bearded, my husband shaved, the way my husband
　　　　　　　taps out the razor, the small hairs
　　　　　　　　　　in the sink.

My husband with tweezers
to my foot,
        to a splinter I carried
for years,
                my husband chiding me
for waiting
to remove what pained me,
        my husband brandishing
                the sliver to the light and laughing.

## The Husband as Saint Sebastian

Some see sacrifice
    where others see torture, and some see suffering
        where others see pleasure.
               You can't control what people make of you.
A body bound and contorted,
    the chest fletched with arrows,
      the inguinal crease
      slashing away from modesty—

of all the martyrs you've loved
      I'm the one who comes
    ripped and rippling to the canvas,
        my face a study in crisis. And you wonder if I like it—

        the way a golden light spills
      over my skin when the head sinks in,
      the way my pain hardens men
        to further action.

Do I ask you how many times
      someone fired an arrow
    your way and you unbuttoned your shirt?
             We've both cast
    our eyes skyward, hoping for release.

Let us have no more
      recriminations.

     You want to know how I can stand
      so long with so little support,
and I'll tell you what I tell myself—
    for God's sake, you just lean into it.

# The Life of the Husband

I think it must look like
>                         the last Dutch elm on the block
dropping its leaves
>               in a yellow carpet on the lawn,
the one I can see from my office window
>           as I am trying to write
>                       some account of my life,
an explanation
>       of how time has taken
>                       to little hops and skips, so fast
now that I'm halfway through
>                       my allotment, and I
>           wanted to say something
>                   about how the morning
>                       limns the grass blades
>           in tiny sheaths of frost, or
that the shingles on the roof
>                       come loose in hard winds
>           and slap the ground
>               like someone
>                       has just said something funny—
I think it must look like
>               the silvery trail
>                   a snail leaves behind
>       on the sidewalk—
>                   the path I've taken—
or the lacy skeleton
>           of a leaf stripped bare,
>               so many branching choices
>               off a central vein,
>           wandering to where
>                       I was going, as if
where I was going
>           was still there.

# ACKNOWLEDGMENTS AND THANKS

Thank you to Mark Stafford, who is always a particular and specific husband. For many secret reasons, this book would not exist without you. We have made a life together of art and words and love.

Thank you to Jimin Seo. In 2021 and 2022, we shared and discussed our work. The poems I wrote and revised during our creative collaboration became this book, and the poems he wrote went on to be published in OSSIA (Changes Press, 2024). Jimin appears in "The Husband Considers Beauty." Jimin adds to the beauty of any street he walks on.

Nancy Reddy and Angela Voras-Hills regularly remind me of everything I love about poetry and friendship. Our AWP was the best AWP, and you both encouraged me to get this book out there.

Over the years, Ron Mitchell and Marcus Wicker at the Southern Indiana Review have repeatedly supported my work, and believed in it when I did not. I cannot thank them enough, on behalf of myself and the poetry community to which they give so much time and energy.

Dr. Jennifer Smith, my colleague and friend, pushed me to apply for an Illinois Arts Council grant. Thank you for that push. Your excitement when I got it was a memory I'll treasure.

Thank you to Jacqueline Osherow for her peer review. It is an extraordinary thing to be read and understood by a powerful poet, and your feedback made this book stronger.

Thank you to James W. Long for giving this book a home.

≈

Several poems from this book were first published in literary magazines and other publications. Thank you for sharing my work, and for the unacknowledged effort and love you give to the literary community. My thanks to the editors of the following publications in which the poems listed first appeared, sometimes in different forms or under different titles: *Adroit Journal:* "The Husband as Mentalist"; *Bennington Review:* "The Husband Proposes"; *Copper Nickel:* "Husband Paraphrase"; *Court Green:* "My Husband"; *Gulf Coast:* "The Husband's Answers [As an abstraction . . .]" and "The Husband's Answers [The images don't explain . . .]"; *iO: A Journal of New American Poetry:* "Apocalypse, Again"; *New Yorker:* "Generic Husband"; *The Pinch:* "Trompe l'Oeil"; *Southern Indiana Review:* "More Husbands" and "The Interior of the Husband"; *Third Coast:* "Epithalamium, Winter Palace"; *Tupelo Quarterly:* "Glazed Case" and "Useful

Tragedy"; *Vinyl Poetry and Prose:* "The Husband Has a Dream"; *Virginia Quarterly Review:* "The Husband as Saint Sebastian," "The Husband as Tilda Swinton in Most Anything," "The Husband with Clothes," and "The Husband without Clothes."

"More Husbands" was also selected by members of the University of Southern Indiana Department of English for the 2022 Mary C. Mohr Award and was published as a broadside.

"My Husband" was also republished in *Best American Poetry 2015.*

≈

Poems from this manuscript were recognized by a Sustainable Arts Foundation award, a Virginia Center for the Creative Arts fellowship, and an Illinois Arts Council grant.

NOTES

"Optimistic Husband" was inspired by several poems containing statuary in Brigit Pegeen Kelly's *The Orchard* (2004), as well as Lady Bertilak's monologue from *The Green Knight* (2021), directed by David Lowery.

"The Husband's Answers" poems reference or draw inspiration from John Berger's *Ways of Seeing* (1972) and Tom Stoppard's *Arcadia* (1993).

"Specific Husband" was written after a long illness from COVID-19.

"Foolish Husbands" is in conversation with "The Fool" from the Rider–Waite tarot deck.

"The Husband as Saint Sebastian" takes inspiration from portraits of the saint. There are so many erotic depictions of St. Sebastian in Western art that no one painting comes to mind, but Guido Reni's *Saint Sebastian* is a good starting point.

www.ingramcontent.com/pod-product-compliance
Ingram Content Group UK Ltd.
Pitfield, Milton Keynes, MK11 3LW, UK
UKHW040635150925
7894UKWH00029B/424

9 780807 184721